This
Treasure Cove Story
belongs to

D0538995

JASMINE IS MY BABYSITTER

A CENTUM BOOK 978-1-912396-69-6
Published in Great Britain by Centum Books Ltd.
This edition published 2018.

3 5 7 9 10 8 6 4 2

Centum Books Ltd, 20 Devon Square, Newton Abbot,
Devon, TQ12 2HR, UK.

www.centumbooksltd.co.uk | books@centumbooksltd.co.uk
CENTUM BOOKS Limited Reg.No. 07641486.

A CIP catalogue record for this book is available
from the British Library.

Printed in China.

centum

A Treasure Cove Story

Jasmine
Is My Babysitter

By Apple Jordan

Illustrated by Mario Cortés and Meritxell Andreu

It was an exciting day in the Kingdom of Agrabah.
The Sultan was expecting some very special guests.

'King Abbud is coming with his children for
a visit,' he told Jasmine. 'The king is an old, dear
friend of mine. It will be wonderful to see him
after all these years.'

At last the king arrived with his family.

'Ah, Abbud, how good to see you!' the Sultan greeted his friend. 'And what a treat it is to meet your lovely children!'

The king tried to introduce Rami, Lina and Hana to the Sultan, but they were too busy running excitedly through the palace.

'Why don't I look after the children?' Jasmine offered. 'I'll show them around so you and my father can have a peaceful visit.'

The king agreed. 'You are very kind,' he said.

The siblings followed Jasmine outside to the garden.

'I come here every morning,' Jasmine said. 'It's my favourite spot in the whole palace.'

'I love it, too!' said Hana, sniffing a rosebush. 'It's beautiful.'

But Rami and Lina were bored. 'Our garden at home is much bigger,' Lina bragged.

Jasmine took them to meet Rajah.

Hana gave the tiger a big hug. 'He's so soft and cuddly!' she said.

'Rajah wouldn't mind taking you for a ride,' Jasmine said.
'But be gentle and only one at a time.'

'We have elephants and camels at home that can give all three
of us a ride at the same time,' Rami boasted.

'Then how about we all take a ride on the Magic Carpet?'
Jasmine suggested.

Soon they were flying high above the village of Agrabah.

'Whee!' yelled Hana. 'This is fun!'

But Rami and Lina were still bored. 'Our magic carpet
at home is faster,' they complained.

'This is tougher than I thought,' Jasmine said
to herself. 'The king's children are hard to please.'

Then she had an idea. Jasmine asked the Genie
for help. He agreed to grant each child one wish.

'Thank you, Genie,' said Jasmine. 'That should
make them happy.' At least, she hoped it would!

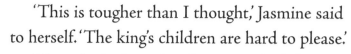

The children were excited when they heard
the news. A wish from a real genie!

Rami knew right away what he wanted. 'I wish for the biggest playground in the world,' he said.

All of a sudden – **POOF!** The Genie turned the Palace Garden into an endless maze of golden swings, slides and jungle gyms. It was the biggest playground the children had ever seen!

'Hooray!' they yelled, running up ladders and sliding down slides.

But when Hana climbed up the biggest slide, she got nervous.
'I can't get down!' she called to Jasmine. 'It's too high!'
'You can do it!' Jasmine coaxed from below.
Hana was too afraid to go.

Jasmine climbed to the top of the slide. 'I'll go down with you,' she said. Hana held on to Jasmine and the two slid down together.

'Thank you for helping me,' she said to Jasmine when they landed at the bottom.

Next it was Lina's turn to make a wish. 'I wish
for all the sweets in the world!' she said.

'Ah, the classic never-ending-sweets wish. That's a tough
one,' the Genie said with a wink, 'but I think I can do it.'

He got to work. **'Allakazam... Allakazoo... ' POOF!**
A giant machine magically appeared. Each time
a button was pushed, a new sweet popped out.

PUSH

The children ate so many sweets, they soon had tummy aches.

'My tummy hurts,' said Hana.

As Jasmine comforted little Hana, she asked the Genie if she could have a wish, too. The Genie agreed.

'I wish for no more sweets,' Jasmine said.

'Good idea,' said the Genie. He waved his arms, and – **POOF!** – the sweet contraption disappeared.

When the children felt better, it was finally Hana's turn.
'I wish… ,' she began.
Everyone was eager to hear her wish. What amazing
thing would she ask for? How big would it be?
'I wish I was just like Jasmine,' she said.

'I'm sorry,' the Genie said, 'but I can't grant that wish.'
'Why not?' Hana asked, disappointed.
'Because you're already like the princess,' said the Genie.
Hana was confused.

'You are kind and caring,' the Genie explained,
'just like Jasmine.'

Jasmine hugged Hana.

'And that means you get to make another wish,'
the Genie told her.

Hana thought and thought.

'I've got it!' she said at last. 'I wish for
the biggest party in the world…'

'...for Jasmine, the best babysitter in the world!'

Treasure Cove Stories

Book list may be subject to change.